Margaret Tempest.

Fuzzypeg Goes to School was first published
in Great Britain by William Collins Sons & Co 1938

This edition published by HarperCollins*Publishers* 2000
Abridged text copyright © The Alison Uttley Literary Property Trust 2000
Illustrations copyright © The Estate of Margaret Tempest 2000
Copyright this arrangement © HarperCollins*Publishers* 2000
Additional illustration by Mark Burgess
Little Grey Rabbit ® and the Little Grey Rabbit logo are
trademarks of HarperCollins*Publishers* Limited

1 3 5 7 9 10 8 6 4 2

ISBN: 000 198407-1

The HarperCollins website address is: www.**fire**and**water**.com

Printed and bound in Singapore

FUZZYPEG GOES TO SCHOOL

ALISON UTTLEY
Pictures by Margaret Tempest

Collins
An Imprint of HarperCollins*Publishers*

IT WAS BEDTIME, and little Fuzzypeg the Hedgehog sat by the fire in his nightgown eating his bread and milk. His mother was mending his blue smock which he had torn on his prickles.

"Will my father tell me a tale tonight?" asked Fuzzypeg.

"If you're a good hedgehog and eat every bit of your supper," said Mrs Hedgehog kindly.

Old Hedgehog came into the cosy room.

"Please tell me a bedtime story," implored Fuzzypeg.

"Wait a minute," said Old Hedgehog, and he
scratched his head, trying to think of a nice tale.

Then he began to sing,

"*A Frog he would a-wooing go,*
Whether his mother would let him or no,
Heigh-ho! says Rowley."

Fuzzypeg beat time with the spoon on the wooden bowl, and Mrs Hedgehog forgot to thread her needle as she listened.

"What a lovely tale!" cried Fuzzypeg.

"I larned that in my schooldays, when I was a youngster," said Hedgehog, modestly.

"Can I go to school and learn poems?" asked Fuzzypeg.

"I think he's big enough, don't you, Hedgehog?" And Mrs Hedgehog looked at her husband.

"Yes. It's about time he had some eddication," replied Hedgehog. "You can't get on without wisdom. Just think what a lot Wise Owl knows!"

"Can I go to school tomorrow? Please! Please!" Fuzzypeg asked, jumping down from his stool.

"Yes, if I've mended these holes in time," Mrs Hedgehog told him.

Fuzzypeg hopped round the room for joy. Then he went to say goodnight to the world.

"Goodnight, Moon," he called to the delicate crescent moon in the sky, and a whispering voice came through the air, "Goodnight, Fuzzypeg."

"Goodnight, Star," he called to the evening star, and it nodded goodnight.

The next morning Fuzzypeg awoke early.

"I'm going to school today," he sang, and he rolled downstairs in a prickly ball.

Old Hedgehog had been out since dawn, milking the cows.

Fuzzypeg saw him returning and ran to meet him. The hedgehog carried something under his arm and Fuzzypeg danced round, asking what it was.

"Don't be in such a hurry," said Old Hedgehog, smiling. He gave Mrs Hedgehog the milk for breakfast, then he sat down and opened the parcel, taking from the leafy paper a little leather bag.

"A school bag!" cried Fuzzypeg excitedly. "A school bag! Where has it come from?"

There was a big pocket for sandwiches, two little ones for lesson books and a tiny one for the penny to pay for the schooling.

"Grey Rabbit gave it to me when she heard you were going to school," said Hedgehog.

"I took the milk as usual this morning, and tells her, 'My Fuzzypeg's going to get Wisdom same as Wise Owl.' 'Wait a minute, Hedgehog,' sez she. So I stood on the doorstep, and then Grey Rabbit comes downstairs, carrying this.

'A lesson bag for Fuzzypeg,' sez she."

"What shall I put in it?" asked Fuzzypeg.

"Your lessons – sums and poems and tales," said Hedgehog, "your sandwiches for elevenses, and your penny for the schoolmaster."

Then they all had a good breakfast, and Fuzzypeg started off for school with the leather bag on his back.

"Don't be late," said his mother, as she waved goodbye.

As Fuzzypeg went down the lane he saw his cousins, Tim and Bill Hedgehog.

"Hello, Fuzzypeg!" they called. "Where are you going with that fine bag?"

"I'm going to school," said Fuzzypeg proudly.

"Wait a minute. We'll come too," cried the little hedgehogs, and they ran to their mother.

"Mother! Mother!" they shouted excitedly. "Can we go to school with Fuzzypeg?"

"Yes. If Fuzzypeg is big enough, so are you," said their mother.

She brushed their quills and cut their sand-wiches, and sent them off.

"Be quick," called Fuzzypeg, "or we'll be late."

"Late? What's late?" asked Tim.

"I don't know. Something we musn't be," replied Fuzzypeg.

They trotted along the lane, when who should they see but Hare, lolloping along in his bright blue coat.

"Hello, Fuzzypeg! Hello, young 'uns!" he called. "What's inside your bag, Fuzzypeg?" he asked.

"Sandwiches," said Fuzzypeg, and he brought them out and divided them.

"Now you have plenty of room for other things," said Hare, and they gathered bindweed, forget-me-nots and foxgloves.

"Those are all lessons," said Hare. "Now I will teach you your A B C."

"A. Hay grows in the Daisy Field, when the sun shines," Hare said.

"B. Bees live in gardens. They get honey and that is a good thing."

"C. Seas are very wet. They are all water and they never dry up."

"That's all for today. You know your A B C," said Hare, suddenly running off, for he had spied little Grey Rabbit coming towards them.

When she saw the three little hedgehogs sitting
on the grass, little Grey Rabbit was astonished.

"What are you doing here, Fuzzypeg?" she
asked. "I thought you were at school. Now run

along as fast as you can, or your teacher will be very cross."

So off they ran, under the gate to the Daisy Field, and across the meadow to the little pasture where Jonathan Rabbit had his school.

A sweet little tinkle tinkle came from the pasture.

"That's the school bell," said a thrush. "You'll be late. Young Hare always rings the harebells, you know. He's been jingling them a long time now."

So they ran, puffing and panting towards the sound of the bluebells, which floated like music from a house hidden in the gorse bushes.

"I've got a stitch in my side," groaned Bill, and he drank from a stream to cure it.

"I've cut my leg on a bramble," cried Tim, and he stopped to find a cobweb to bind up the wound.

"I've tored my smock on the gorse bush," said Fuzzypeg, and he looked for a thorn to pin it together.

In the distance the little hare stood in a grove
of slender harebells, shaking the bells for the
last time.

Then he ran into school, and there was silence.

The three hedgehogs raced to the school door. They pushed aside a leafy curtain, and knocked at the little green door with a brass knocker, hidden in the low bushes.

Then they entered a room whose walls were made of closely woven blackberry bushes and wild roses.

The floor was the soft turf of the pasture, and the ceiling of the schoolroom was the blue sky, where the sun was now shining. The little hedgehogs walked shyly across the room to old Jonathan.

"Benjamin Hedgehog. Timothy Hedgehog. Fuzzypeg Hedgehog," said he, writing their names on a rose leaf, in squiggly letters.

"Each of you is, 'A diller, a dollar, a ten-o'clock scholar.' Remember that school begins at nine o'clock, and don't be late!"

They sat down next to hedgehogs, squirrels, rabbits, the young hare, a small mole and some fieldmice. They all read from books made of green leaves which Jonathan gave them.

Then he asked them some questions, and all the little animals stood up in a row, with Fuzzypeg at the end.

"Which flower helps a rabbit to remember?" he asked.

Nobody knew the answer, but little Fuzzypeg drew
the blue forget-me-nots from his bag and held
them up.

"Quite right, Fuzzypeg. Go to the top of the class," said Jonathan.

"Which flower shuts its eyes when it rains?" he asked.

All the little animals shut their eyes and tried forget-me-notting, but Fuzzypeg held up the white trumpet of the climbing bindweed.

Then Jonathan asked his last question.

"Which flower makes gloves for cold paws?"

Every animal knew the answer, and they all shouted at the tops of their voices, "Foxgloves," before Fuzzypeg could get the purple foxglove from the bottom of his satchel.

"Now for a counting lesson," said Jonathan.

"One, two, buckle my shoe," sang the animals, and all the little hedgehogs fastened their shoes.

"Three, four, knock at the door," they sang, and they ran to knock on the brass knocker.

"Five, six, pick up sticks," they sang, and they all ran into the pasture to gather as many sticks as they could carry.

"Seven, eight, lay them straight," they sang, and each tried to lay his sticks in even lengths.

"Eleven o'clock," said Jonathan, blowing at a dandelion clock. "Go and eat your sandwiches."

Fuzzypeg had nothing to eat, but there was plenty of fun and he played leapfrog with the others up and down the soft grass.

Suddenly Fuzzypeg saw a little figure in a grey dress coming towards the school.

"Here's little Grey Rabbit!" called all the animals, and they rushed to meet her, and begged her to tell them a story.

Little Grey Rabbit sat down in the shade of a hawthorn tree, and began the tale of Red Riding Hood. She had just got to the part where Red Riding Hood came to her grandmother's cottage, when there was a mighty roaring noise close by, from behind the hawthorn tree.

"Woof! Woof! Woof!" said a terrible voice.

"Oh! Oh!" they all shrieked. "Oh! the Wolf!"

And they all ran helter-skelter up and down the field.

Grey Rabbit stood very still, for she thought she
recognised the voice.

"Boo! Boo! Woof! Woof! I'll nab you," roared
the creature, gruffly.

"Come out, Hare," said Grey Rabbit sternly.

"Hare! Naughty Hare! Come out at once! I know that voice. You can't deceive *me*."

From behind the tree leaped Hare, holding a cone-shaped trumpet, made from the bark of a silver birch tree.

"Ha! Ha! I frightened you. You thought it was a Wolf, didn't you?"

All the little animals came creeping out, to stare at the trumpet which Hare carried; all, except Fuzzypeg.

"Where's Fuzzypeg?" asked little Grey Rabbit.

"Where's Fuzzypeg?" echoed the others.

Then they heard a squeaky little voice.

"A-tishoo!" it said. "Help! A-tishoo! A-shoo!"

From out of the stream crawled a very bedraggled little hedgehog, all covered with water weeds.

"C is very wet," he said. "A-tishoo!"

"Poor little Fuzzypeg," said Grey Rabbit, running up to him. "You'd better go straight home to bed."

"School, dismissed!" shouted Jonathan.

All the little animals leaped up and down crying, "A holiday!"

"I didn't want a holiday. I've only just begun," said Fuzzypeg in a quavering voice. "A-tishoo!"

But Grey Rabbit took him by the hand, and hurried him home, while Hare ran alongside.

"I'll give you the trumpet, Fuzzypeg," said he. "Then you can be a wolf, or even a lion."

This cheered Fuzzypeg so much he forgot about missing school, and wetting his new school bag.

"Whatever have you been and gone and done?" asked Mrs Hedgehog, holding up her hands in horror when she saw her wet little son.

Little Grey Rabbit explained what had happened, and Hare said, "I'm very sorry, Mrs Hedgehog. It won't occur again." Then he ran off, leaping home.

"You must put Fuzzypeg to bed at once, Mrs Hedgehog," said Grey Rabbit.

So little Fuzzypeg was popped into his warm bed, with a bowl of delicious soup and blackcurrant tea.

Grey Rabbit sat at his bedside and she sang little songs to him while Fuzzypeg sneezed and sneezed again. On the wall hung the trumpet, and when Grey Rabbit blew it, a roaring noise came from it which made Fuzzypeg laugh.

When little Grey Rabbit started for home, Fuzzypeg croaked, "Good-bye, Grey Rabbit."

And then he shut his eyes and slept till his father came home.

"What did they larn you besides swimming, my son?" asked Old Hedgehog, as he stood at the bedside looking at little Fuzzypeg, muffled up in his blankets.

"Hay, Bee and Sea. I think that was what Hare taught us. I fell into C, Father. And tomorrow we're going to learn, 'Here we go gathering nuts in May.' I like school, Father."

"You've not larned much," said Old Hedgehog, "and they say, 'A little larning is a dangerous thing.' You'd better get a bit more knowledge tomorrow, and don't go to Mr Hare for your lessons neither."